10 Stories to Make a Difference is a collection of ten original illustrated stories for young readers, all inspired by the theme of *difference*. The collection features a mix of well-known and emerging writers and illustrators, giving a platform to untold stories and diverse new voices. Produced by Pop Up Projects, a non-profit, UK-based national children's literature development agency, 10 Stories celebrates Pop Up's 10th birthday in 2021. Proceeds from sales supports Pop Up's work in deprived schools, marginalised communities, and with talented writers and illustrators, especially from backgrounds that are under-represented in children's publishing. 10 Stories will be an annual publishing event, with a whole new collection planned for 2022.

Find out more at **www.pop-up.org.uk**

Jamila Gavin is a writer of Anglo-Indian heritage who emigrated to Britain as a child. She's been publishing children's books for all ages since 1979, often inspired by the changing face of multicultural Britain, and driven by a desire to see children of all backgrounds reflected in the stories they read. Jamila's books include the *Grandpa Chatterji* series, *The Surya Trilogy* and *Blackberry Blue.* Her historical novel *Coram Boy*, set in 18th century England, won the Whitbread Children's Book of the Year, is in development with BBC TV, adapted by National Theatre and had run on Broadway.

Jacinta Read is a Eurasian illustrator and writer whose work is influenced by her love of dance and old musicals. As a neurodivergent child who struggled to read, it was illustration that opened up the wonderful world of literature to her; she hopes her pictures will do the same for others. Jacinta lives in Oxford with her husband, two children, and Louie the red Jack Russell. She's an illustration mentee on Pop Up's Pathways into Children's Publishing programme (2019-2021). *In Her Element* is Jacinta's first published children's book.

Edited by **Liz Bankes**, Farshore
Art directed by **Tiffany Leeson**, Farshore

Publisher **Dylan Calder**
Coordinator **Amanda Saakwa-Mante**
Designer **Txabi Jones**

IN HER ELEMENT

Written by
Jamila Gavin

Illustrated by
Jacinta Read

04 55: Sophie awoke and flung out her arms. She leapt out of bed. The sea was calling her. Time for a swim. Before she knew it, she had on her jeans, anorak and trainers, and, with her swimming costume and towel stuffed into a rucksack, was skipping along a sun-sprinkled leafy lane towards the sea.

There it was! The sea; an almost unbearable blue, piercing through the branches ahead. She raced across the downs to the cliff edge. Sophie felt she could leap into space and fly, taking the steep path winding down to the shore below. The screeching gulls whirled around, and the crashing waves splattered her with spray. Far out to sea, she spotted a school of dolphins, their bodies arching through the waves like slurs on a page of music.

Suddenly, Sophie glimpsed a familiar figure. It was herself; as she imagined herself; standing on the headland looking out to sea. The sky was rich blue behind her, and clouds swept across like white hair blown in the wind. She was tall and lean; her body as aerodynamic as a fish, legs tightly together; she raised her arms and dived into the ocean.

05.00: Sophie half opened her eyes. Dawn hadn't yet broken. She thought about the heaving sea; feeling its vast force raising her up on to the peaks of the waves and dropping her down into the troughs. She sometimes thought, in another time, she had been someone else, or something else: a fish; the Little Mermaid, perhaps, or a whale. Yes, she liked the idea of being a whale. When her carer, Martin, had asked her when they first met; "what is your element?" she remembered blinking at him, puzzled. "You know," he said, "there are four elements: earth, air, fire and water; mine's earth. I love to feel the ground beneath my feet – so that won't be you, will it!"

Martin could always speak the truth without inflicting pain, and she had laughed uproariously, and immediately replied with her word chart. "Water." She hadn't even had to think about it.

Her body was strapped into her bed as usual to stop her limbs moving without her control and, like the Little Mermaid she had no voice – except grunts and screeches. Yet, sometimes, she was sure she had some kind of memory

of when she had the use of her body: like her brother, Freddy, like her parents, like almost everyone who came into the house.

Perhaps in another life, she had been a fish. Her body often told her so, and she was always dreaming about swimming in heaving oceans, being lifted up on giant waves and, like surfers, riding them down with the crest curling like serpents behind her. She loved it when they took her swimming and, though strapped into a hoist, she imagined she lived in an underwater kingdom, where her body had motion; where her spine eddied like a rudder and her limbs moved – not as humans move – but like a fish – and that she could sing.

Time stood poised like a diver on the end of a diving board, ready to plunge into the next day. "Water is my element," she repeated.

"Good." Martin had smiled. "Earth and Water are like brother and sister."

She could hear the radio coming from her parents' bedroom right next door. Freddy was laughing. He had awoken, and run to get into bed with Mum and Dad. Dear little brother Freddy; who, although he was only three and was only just learning to talk himself, was the one who understood what Sophie wanted faster than anyone else. Likewise, long before Freddy could talk properly, she understood him.

She gazed at herself in the broad mirror nearby and she paused, looking at herself: at her pale oval face – like the Mona Lisa, people said, because there always seemed to be the trace of a smile, as if she knew something no one else did.

But most of all, people were drawn to her eyes. Sophie looked into her own eyes now, those large, expressive nut-brown eyes which could dance with laughter, or glower with frustration.

Having no power to speak, she communicated with her eyes: opening, closing, how fast, how slow; narrowing, widening, blinking one for yes, two for no, lifting and lowering her eyebrows, expressing pleasure, frustration, understanding or impatience, her laser accurate gaze focusing on the objects she required, or which helped to express her need.

Beyond the mirror, through the window, her eyes climbed into the cherry tree which was in full bridal bloom, and roamed across the layers of hazy hills. Her ears followed her eyes and listened: she was sure that she could hear the roar of the sea, the sucking rattle of pebbles on the shore, the scream of seagulls, and a whale singing.

"If I were a whale… If… wish…"

06 15: Her mother came in.

"Sophie darling, how are you today?" She drew the curtains, and sunshine poured in. "The weather forecast says it will rain, so we'd better make the most of the morning." She chattered cheerfully as she held a bottle of orange juice with a straw to Sophie's mouth.

Her father suddenly came into the room. His face was solemn, and her mother's expression changed from a cheery grin to anxious concern.

"Sophie," her mother kissed her forehead.

"We have news for you," said Dad, stroking her arm.

They spoke, alternating with each other as they always did.

"I do hope you'll be pleased," said Mum.

"We've talked about it for a long time…" said Dad

"I know you enjoy going to school here …"

"And Martin is brilliant... but..."

"You're older now. Your needs are changing."

"Remember that school we went round last spring?"

"Allandale."

"They've just written to say they can offer you a place – starting next term."

"It's rather short notice. But we think you're ready and that you shouldn't miss this chance. It's awfully difficult to get in; such a demand for places."

"It means leaving home; it's residential of course."

"And we've been reassured that they can meet all your needs with equipment, as well as trained staff. They say you'll be fine."

"We'll miss you like hell – but it's for the best."

"You'll be more independent."

"You'll find a way of using all your talents."

"You're such a brave, beautiful, intelligent young woman."

"Yes, the time has come."

"It's time you left home."

That's how they spoke, each overlapping with the other; each wanting to sound positive and full of hope.

"Sophie? Do you want to give it a try?"

"Of course, if you're unhappy, we'll bring you home and think of something else."

"But we need to plan now. We're all getting older."

That was their way of saying, one day, we'll be too old to look after you; one day we'll die, and then what will happen?

It seemed the ocean flooded into the house. Her room shimmered. A cluster of tiny fish spun past like molecules, all making up one fish. A large goggle-eyed creature, with flabby pouting lips slowly floated by, with just odd twitches of his fins to propel him along; a disembodied triangle came through the door towards her parents and circled them.

"Shark! Look out!" She wanted to cry, but with a flick, the fin disappeared through the half-open window. She felt a powerful watery tremor as it passed by, and the brief flutter from the end of its tail which brushed her cheek; for a moment; no longer than the blink of an eye or the flare of a match.

And then a huge presence engulfed the house; whale! An explosive shriek broke from her throat, before it too was gone. Sophie's head hurled backwards against the headrest. "Don't go!"

"What do you think, Sophie? Give it a try, eh?"

—

The radio was full of more reports about the stranded

whale. A reporter described seeing a number of whales which seemed to have gathered out at sea, moving together as in some kind of dance, circling, plunging and leaping above the waves, emitting long searing notes interspersed with shorter clicks, as if communicating with each other. The reporter had recorded their songs, and excitedly played back the sound. "I've heard of the song of the whales," the reporter exclaimed excitedly, "but I never thought it could be anything like this."

"They're not just songs," Sophie found herself screaming inside.

"They're words, they're speaking – and I understand. I am a whale."

She glanced out of the window, and saw a bird flying backwards.

Martin came into the room, jaunty as a comedian. He stopped smiling when he saw her face.

"Are you OK?"

"I'm going away." Sophie had already put the words up on her screen for Martin to read when he came to take her to school.

"I'm going away," Martin read out loud, "to a boarding school for people like me, called Allandale." Then tears were streaming down her face.

"Oh. So, they've told you.
I didn't think it would be so soon." Martin gave her a quick hug. He read on. "What shall I do without you?"

she had written. Martin took out his hanky and wiped away her tears.

"Why, you'll do fine. I was already beginning to feel superfluous. You've got a brain as good as Einstein, you're as stubborn as a mule, and you have the determination of – who *was* that young woman who went round the world solo on her yacht? – you know, her. Anyway – I thought you wanted to take your A-levels, go to university and be a writer. My goodness, you've more ambition than I ever had!"

Sophie thrust her head forward so that she could spell out more words. "Why can't I do those things here, with you?"

Martin helped her to blow her nose. "You've got to learn to be independent. You've got to learn to be on your own; take control of your life. No one will abandon you. There'll always be someone there for you, Sophie. All this will come clear to you – just you see. You will be happier, more than you ever dreamed of. Believe me, going to this school will make all the difference."

Through the window, Sophie saw a whale flick its tail into the setting sun, and an unexpected wind swirled through the trees, tossing the branches about as if battered by invisible waves.

–

The sky was as clear and shining as the surface of an eye, even though a single, grey, sleek, whale-like cloud dominated the horizon, and seemed to be keeping pace with them.

"Are you all right, sweetie?" asked her father, glancing at her in the rear mirror. "It won't be long now."

She blinked hard.

"You'll be fine," her father reassured her.

–

"Ah so this is Sophie! Welcome Sophie, I'm Barbara Maplin, your key worker here at Allandale," she welcomed them with warm smiles. "Call me Bussie! Everyone does. As we discussed, you are sharing a room with Amber Taylor. Till your own room becomes available. So sorry about that. But I'm hopeful that your love of water means you and Amber will be friends, and help each other."

But after a week at Allendale; a week when Sophie felt she would die of homesickness; Amber had still shown no signs of being her friend. She was bitter and unfriendly. An accident had put an end to her dream of being an Olympic swimmer. She was terrified and angry.

"Oh! You're one of those!"

she remarked on realizing Sophie was non verbal.

Sophie stared, unsure how to respond, then wrote, "Sorry."

Amber shrugged and wheeled herself away.

–

Before Sophie's parents left, they had asked Amber if she minded them displaying Sophie's family photographs, and if they could pin up the poster of the whale Martin had given her. Sophie noticed a small fading photograph pinned above Amber's desk, almost hidden between a silky cocker spaniel,

and a cute little kitten with a pink bow. It was of a young, slim, long-legged, athletic girl, shining black, standing on a high diving board. Her toes curled over the edge, her arms outstretched in parallel above her head, her eyes raised upwards in total concentration. With a shock, Sophie realised it was Amber.

"Yeh! That's me last year, seconds before I dived in and my dream ended. It was a hotel pool on holiday. They didn't tell me they hadn't finished filling it."

There was another photograph next to it: Amber and an athletic-looking lad, handsome as a god, their arms draped around each other. But Amber didn't refer to it. She turned her back on Sophie. "I've an assignment to get done."

—

Sophie emailed Martin: "My roommate's called Amber. She was everything I'd like to have been: a wonderful swimmer, tall and beautiful. It's so much worse for her. I was born as I am and, because I lost nothing that I was born with, I have everything to gain and look forward to. Whereas she was born with everything, and was in her prime, when she lost it all in an accident. Isn't life strange? I don't think she'll be my friend. In fact, I think she hates me. I thought I would feel normal here, but I don't. I still feel different. I'm so lonely. Come and visit me soon."

"There is a creature which is cocooned beneath the earth in utter darkness," Martin had told her once. "Then when its inner clock chimes 'ready!' it crawls out into the sun and, in one frantic joyous day, it lives: flying, flirting, mating; its body, its senses – its entire reason for being part of the universe, fulfilled.

Cocooned in her bed Sophie felt like that creature; lying patiently, as if waiting for her day; waiting for her escape into that ecstatic freedom when she would go flying and swimming with the whales.

But where did Amber want to be? At night, Sophie listened to Amber in her bed across the room, thrashing from side to side; moaning in her sleep. Her first night had been the most strange and disturbing night Sophie had ever had. She had never slept away from home before, and she could scarcely breathe for the suffocating weight of homesickness in her stomach.

In the nightlight-blue darkness, Amber's incoherent mumblings became clearer: "You do love me, don't you? I am your one and only. Where are you going Jase? Can I come too? It doesn't matter about my legs, does it? I'm still beautiful, aren't I?" And so she whispered, and sobbed in her sleep.

–

Sophie soon met Amber's friends.

Two girls in wheelchairs manoeuvred themselves into the room, struggling and giggling, forcing Sophie to the side to make way for them.

"She your new roommate?" They talked about her as if she wasn't there.

"Yeh!" Amber replied in a bored voice. "Her name's Sophie."

"Hi Sophie!" They turned to her at last with frantic friendly waves.

Sophie squawked and flashed her eyes.

"She can't talk," shrugged Amber in a 'not worth bothering with her,' kind of voice, so they didn't. Sophie flashed her eyes again, hoping someone would try and communicate with her or show just one flicker of connection, but they didn't, and she felt herself becoming invisible. They were already in a huddle, leaning out of their wheelchairs, sharing pics on their phones, and talking about boys.

"How's Jason then?" asked one, glancing meaningfully at the photograph on the wall, of Amber and a young man. "Is he going to be at the gig?"

"Yeah . . ." giggled Amber. "Hey guys! What are you going to wear, eh?" and they plunged into a discussion about clothes and makeup.

Feeling like a trespasser, Sophie wheeled out of the room and away to the entrance hall. She would like to have gone out through the automatic front doors, down the avenue, on and on until she reached the ocean, or the end of the world.

When Amber and her friends had gone, she emailed Martin.

"I've missed you all, and I haven't made a friend yet. Amber is like two people: Amber by day, when she is joking with her friends, and planning what to wear to their next gig, and Amber by night, when she tosses and turns and weeps in her sleep. I thought I would be in my element here. I thought I'd be with people like me, and that they would understand me and be my friend. But there's nobody like me. Bussie's kind, and my teachers are patient. I really like them. But they're not like you, Martin. No one talks about whales, or Time, or the Universe as you do. Amber, isn't at all interested. Probably can't wait for me to move to my own room."

"What element do you think Amber is?" Martin emailed her back.

The obvious element would be water, as she had been a champion swimmer, and yet Sophie felt Amber's element was fire; not a blazing, fiercely hot fire, but a slow, smouldering, ash-suffocated fire, slowly dying unless something could revive her. So, she put the word "fire," up on her screen.

"Hmmm," sighed Martin, "perhaps you're right.

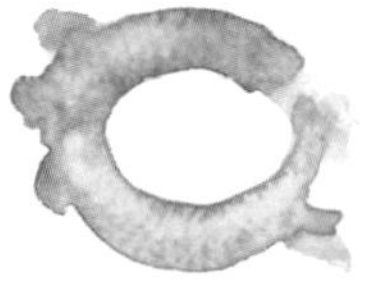

She's certainly burnt your fingers. Seems fire and water may not go together."

He sent her a YouTube link of whales leaping and swimming and singing. One swam so close to the camera she could look deep into its eye. It was like staring into a black hole. She felt as if she could be sucked right down inside and discover a whole new universe; or maybe arrive somewhere before the Big Bang. Martin liked to talk about blackholes, wormholes and the string theories; that there could be all sorts of other universes existing in different time planes?

Time.

If only I could go into whale time, she thought and, as she daydreamed, she transformed: her body became like a whale's body, a sound chamber, communicating stereophonically through two aural mechanisms which amplified whale sound and vibrations, coiling and interweaving in her head with clicks, wails, moans, and vowels.

Outside, a thunderstorm broke, but Sophie was already swimming in the ocean, streaking at great speed, her graceful tail flukes flipping like giant wings, her muscles and skin, oscillating with joy. Sensations of sound rippled over her body as she followed the singing whales. She swam faster and faster along the songline, occasionally hurtling up to the surface and leaping ecstatically high, and arched, her full whale body clear of the waves before crashing down.

Sophie had gone to the open window to see the storm. Now she sat, her head thrown back, her eyes closed. Her computer still flickered with a kind of musical stave on which incomprehensible wavy lines peaked and troughed like the sea. Her face was a strange bluish grey pallor like that of a whale or dolphin.

"Sophie? Sophie!"

Amber's panicky voice

hooked her like a fishing line and pulled her back.

Sophie opened her eyes.

"You gave me a shock sitting there so still." Amber's voice was accusing.

"Let me go!" Sophie's eyebrows rose and fell desperately. "I want to stay in the ocean." Her face was wet with millions of droplets sparkling in her hair and clothes.

"Look at you! The window's open! You're soaked! Let's get you sorted!" Amber wheeled to the bathroom and brought back a towel. She dried off Sophie's face. "Anyone would think you'd been dunked in the ocean. What on earth were you thinking?"

Amber stared at her puzzled; perhaps concerned; Sophie returned her gaze. "Can't we be friends?"

There was the faintest flicker, then it was gone.

"Must get ready for the gig tonight," and Amber turned away.

It was after midnight, when the door burst open. Amber wheeled in full of chatter and excitement. "Ssssh!" she chastised herself. "Mustn't wake Sophie!"

But Amber couldn't "Ssssh" herself. She was a little tipsy. "There was a brilliant boy band, and canapes and drinks – and Jason! My lovely Jason! He danced with me the whole time; whirled me about under all those strobing, flashing, coloured lights. I shall have that on my wedding day. Whoops! I'm waking you up. Sorry Sophie!" She clapped her hand over her mouth, and grinned, but prattled on while she got ready for bed.

Sophie lay still as a stone.

"Night, night Sophie!" Amber chirped, "Light going out!" She clicked off the light. "I could have danced all night!" she sang softly.

Wide awake, Sophie breathed deeply; she lay in a dark sea cave smelling of wet seaweed.

Amber's mobile beeped in the darkness alerting her to a text. She groped under her pillow,

and her face was lit by the light of her phone. "Jase! What kind of time is this to text me!" she exclaimed with a pleased giggle.

There was a sudden intake of breath. The pause extended and extended as if she would never breathe again. Sophie waited; then it came; the heaving, gulping, choking sobs. Amber howled.

Sophie listened helplessly; unable to even stretch out a hand. She had to lie, long into the night, and listen to Amber crying. Finally, Amber reached across to Sophie and held out the illumined face of her mobile phone. Sophie read it:

Wanted to tell you tonight, but couldn't. Sorry. You must know that we were never going to work. Things change: time moves on; I'm not worthy of you, Amb. You need someone better than me. I think a clean break is the best. I'll never forget you. Good luck for the future. Jase. Xxx

"Coward. Coward, coward! Couldn't tell me face to face," and, with a single press, Amber deleted it, sobbing desperately.

Sophie screeched and thrashed about to attract Amber's attention. She looked as if she were trying to hurl herself from her bed. Amber sat up, still weeping, yet alarmed by Sophie's agitation. She put on the light, and Sophie used all her power to tell Amber she needed her computer to write a message.

At last Amber understood.

"Okay, okay!" She sniffed angrily, and wriggled herself out of bed. Like a mermaid, she slithered across the floor and heaved herself first into her wheelchair, then reached for Sophie's. Getting her into her wheelchair would be tricky. "Are you sure you want to do this? What if I drop you?"

Sophie squawked and grunted emphatically.

"Good to know my arms are still strong," said Amber, heaving Sophie from the bed and flopping her into her wheelchair. "Sorry! You're all of a heap," she gasped.

Amber wheeled her over to the computer and switched it on. Sophie raised her head to focus her gaze. Two words gleamed on the screen. "Amber Swim."

"What me?" Amber screeched with derision. "You must be joking. Do you think I ever want to go near water again – ever? I told them that when I came. That's why they've left me alone. So, don't you start."

More words gleamed on Sophie's screen.

"Swim, swim. Water."

The swimming pool. Amber knew that Sophie liked to go to the Allendale pool; that they lifted her into a hoist and lowered her into the water. It was her one great joy.

Sophie's face was white, her eyes large; shining; pleading; speaking more than any words could. Amber knew she was urging, over and over again. "Let's go swimming."

Sophie knew no one had persuaded Amber to get back into the water. The more they had said things like "think positive," the more she had screamed: "Do you understand me? I will never go into water ever again." And Sophie knew that the break-up with Jason had left her humiliated; he had confirmed her greatest fear; that she counted for nothing and would always count for nothing.

"Let's do it. Let's go. Now."

Sophie gave a gentle grunt of encouragement, but not strapped in, she was sliding perilously down her chair.

Amber heaved Sophie from under her armpits till she was more or less sitting straight in her chair.

Sophie threw back her head and laughed.

"Ssssh!" hissed Amber, and doubled up with muffled laughter herself. "You'll wake someone!" But they both giggled.

"Sssssh!" Amber opened the door, and the two of them wheeled out into the dim silent corridor and down towards the swimming pool.

Amber shivered; she smelt the chlorine; she saw the vast blue still water stretching down the length of the pool, the reflected lights glittering like stars, and the red lines of the lanes refracting under the soft light.

Sophie wheeled down to the deep end while Amber stared at the element which had once been her life; had contained all her dreams, and given her happiest moments of triumph and success. Her whimpers rose higher and higher and bitter tears coursed down her cheeks.

"Get it into your head, Sophie, I'll never swim again. Never. This was a stupid thing to do. I'm going back to bed." As she angrily spun round, turning her back on the pool, she heard the softest 'splosh.'

She whirled herself round. Where was Sophie? In a kind of daze, she stared down the length of the pool, disbelieving: Sophie and her wheelchair had toppled into the swimming pool and were slowly sinking. In the blue light she felt as if she were by the

open sea, and that it was the heavens with all its stars and planets which reflected around her.

Amber stared; mesmerized; fearful. What could she do? Run away? How long did it take? Two… three seconds? Amber's fingers stroked the controls. She released the brakes, and accelerated. Her wheel chair thrust forward with a whirring, hovered for a tenth of a second on the brink, and hurtled into the water.

She released herself from the chair and, with a twist of her body, her arms powered her down the length of the pool, her helpless legs trailing behind. She saw Sophie, below her, with face upturned, and hair streaming like seaweed, her eyes wide, ecstatic, as if staring at the cosmos, with a look of utter joy on her face as her body began to lift from the chair and float away.

Amber plunged underwater. It seemed to be swirling with tones, semitones and harmonics as shoals of strange fish circled her; with chuckles and tuts and clicks, as dolphins dipped and dived in bubbles of air; and crystals bursting with a million trillion universes.

She clasped Sophie's chin with one hand and, with her free arm, lashed out for the surface, feeling she had only just held her back from disappearing down some deep blue abyss which seemed to open up beneath them.

She lunged towards the ramp at the shallow end of the pool and thrust Sophie up the slope, then pulled herself up alongside her.

They lay, panting and gasping side by side like mermaids.

"What the hell did you think you were doing, Sophe?"

Sophie gave a wild shriek of joy, and then they both laughed. They laughed and laughed and laughed, and laughed, as though they had just discovered laughter; laughter which ricocheted round all the oceans of the world…on…and on.. and on.

Amber's element was water.

For Jeb, whose joy, intelligence, and friendship was such an inspiration (Jamila)

For Layla (Jacinta)

For Olive, for lighting up our lives with your sunshine smiles, and for Holi and BJ, for bringing her into the world (Dylan)

Thank You!

The 10 Stories collection has been made possible through the generosity and love poured into these stories by our old friends and new, the writers and illustrators who all gave their wisdom and magic: Philip Ardagh, Avital Balwit, Jamie Beard, Sita Brahmachari, Eleanor Cullen, Danica Da Silva Pereira, Ria Dastidar, Alexis Deacon, Laura Dockrill, Jamila Gavin, Sahar Haghgoo, Jay Hulme, Daniel Ido, Krista M. Lambert, Jane Ray, Jacinta Read, Chris Riddell, David Roberts, Marcus Sedgwick, Anjali Tiwari. And through the kindness and devotion of the brilliant publishing editors, art directors and designers who volunteered their time to transform these great stories into even greater books: Emily Ball, Liz Bankes, Andrew Biscomb, Jane Buckley, Alice Curry, Holly Fulbrook, Lilly Gottwald, Elorine Grant, Libby Hamilton, Daisy Jellicoe, Txabi Jones, Ruth Knowles, Tiffany Leeson, Jacqui McDonough, Caroline Royds, Chloé Tartinville, Holly Tonks, Clare Whitston, Sean Williams. Huge gratitude to Matt Baxter and Lydia Fisher at Baxter & Bailey for donating their time to produce the 10 Stories brand, style and formats. If it wasn't for the 643 donors to our crowdfunding campaign, these books may never have made it to print - and we especially want to thank Rachel Denwood and Simon & Schuster, Sam Arthur and Nobrow, Michelle McLeod and Baillie Gifford, the CSR team at Linklaters LLP, Tim Bevan, Wolfgang Tillmans and all our former Board members for their generous support. Behind the scenes, the team and Board at Pop Up kept this great ship afloat through these most turbulent times, and we cannot thank them enough for always being part of the story no matter how hard the story gets.

Made possible by

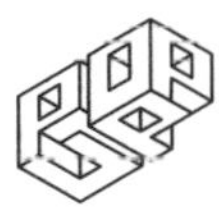

Baxter & Bailey

Farshore

This is a first edition. First published in Great Britain in 2021 by Pop Up Projects CIC 5 City Garden Row London N1 8DW. Printed and bound in Poland by Ozgraf www.ozgraf.com.pl ISBN 978-1-8383-2359-2

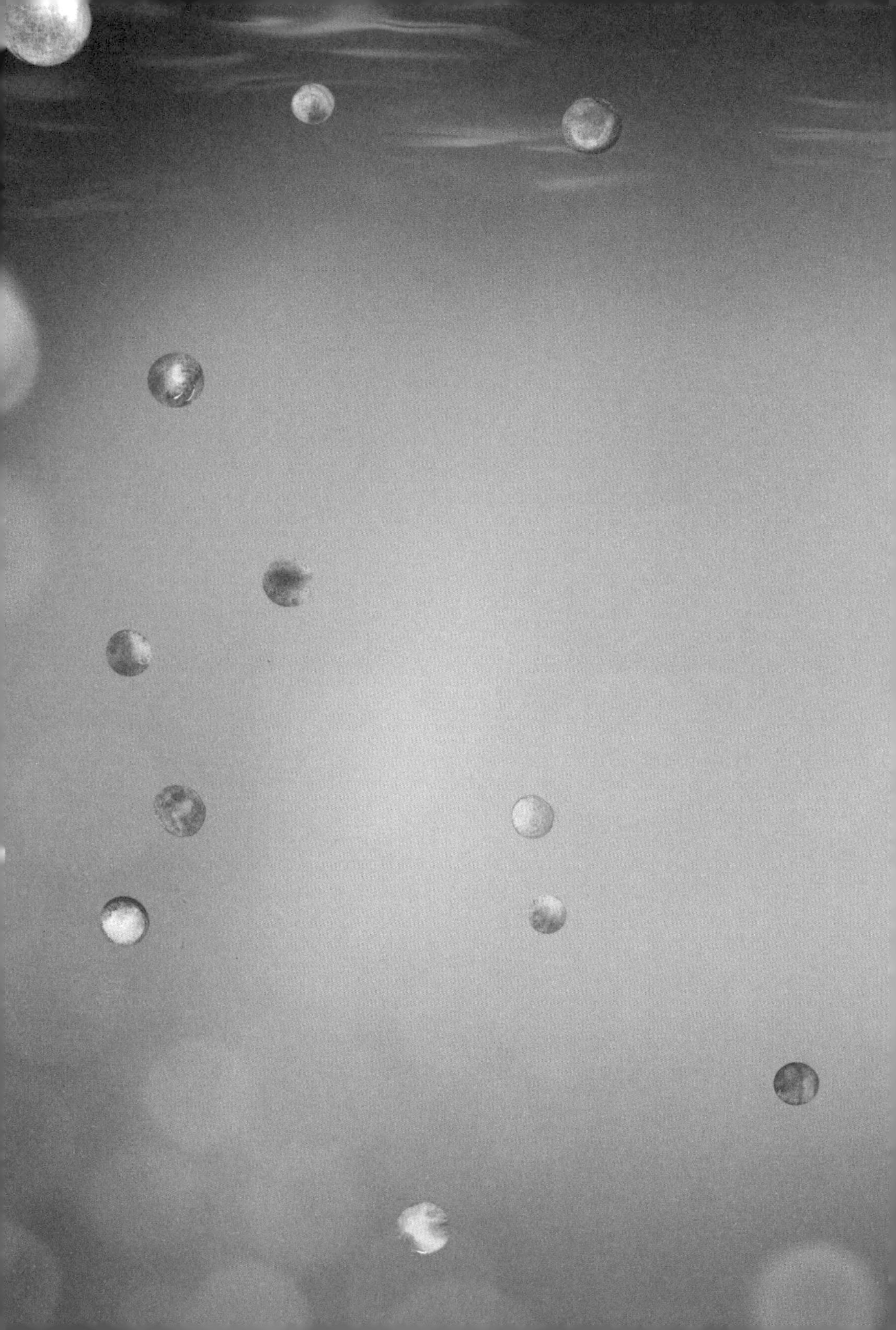